W9-BMJ-583
DISCARD

LOOK FOR THESE OTHER
TITLES IN THIS SERIES

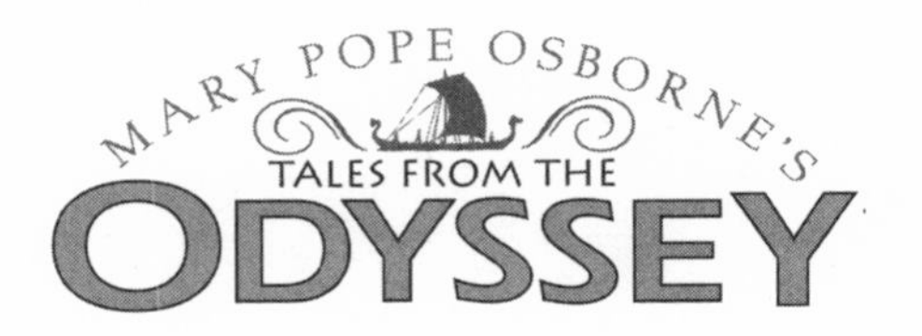

BOOK ONE
THE ONE-EYED GIANT

BOOK TWO
THE LAND OF THE DEAD

BOOK THREE
SIRENS AND SEA MONSTERS

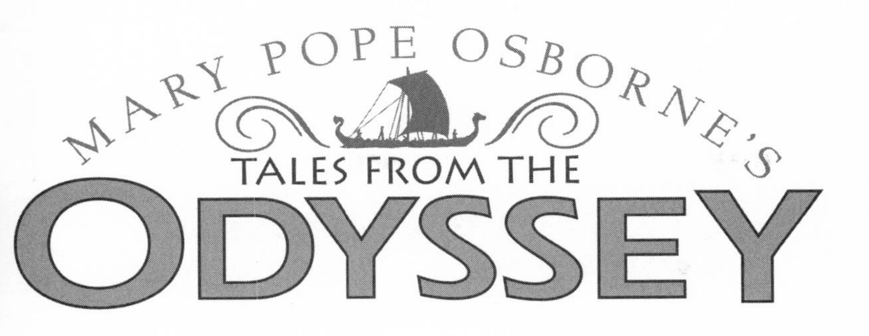

Book Four

THE GRAY-EYED GODDESS

By MARY POPE OSBORNE
With artwork by TROY HOWELL

LAKE AGASSIZ REGIONAL LIBRARY
118 S. 5th St. Box 900
MOORHEAD, MINNESOTA 56561-0900

Hyperion Books for Children New York

Special thanks to Frederick J. Booth, Ph.D.,
Professor of Classical Studies, Seton Hall University,
for his expert advice

Text copyright © 2003 by Mary Pope Osborne
Artwork copyright © 2003 by Troy Howell
All rights reserved. No part of this book may be reproduced or transmitted in any form or by any means, electronic or mechanical, including photocopying, recording, or by any information storage and retrieval system, without written permission from the publisher. For information address Hyperion Books for Children, 114 Fifth Avenue, New York, New York 10011-5690.

First Edition

1 3 5 7 9 10 8 6 4 2

Printed in the United States of America
Library of Congress Cataloging-in-Publication Data on file.
ISBN 0-7868-0773-3
Visit www.hyperionchildrensbooks.com

To Gail Hochman

CONTENTS

PROLOGUE

In the early morning of time, there existed a mysterious world called Mount Olympus. Hidden behind a veil of clouds, this world was never swept by winds, nor washed by rains. Those who lived on Mount Olympus never grew old; they never died. They were not humans. They were the mighty gods and goddesses of ancient Greece.

The Olympian gods and goddesses had great power over the lives of the humans who lived on earth below. Their anger once caused a man named Odysseus to wander the seas for many long years, trying to find his way home.

Almost three thousand years ago, a Greek poet named Homer first told the story of Odysseus' journey. Since that time, story-tellers have told the strange and wondrous tale again and again. We call that story the Odyssey.

ONE

ODYSSEUS AND PENELOPE

Odysseus, king of Ithaca, walked slowly along the shore of the wooded island. As he stared at the restless sea, he yearned for his distant homeland. He had not seen his island of Ithaca, or his family, for almost twenty years—not since he had sailed away to fight in the Trojan War. He mourned his ill luck since the war's end.

Perhaps I would be home in Ithaca now, he thought, *if the Greeks had not angered Athena, the warrior goddess, and caused our ships to be blown off course . . . or if I had not angered Poseidon, the god of the seas, by blinding his son, the Cyclops . . . or if my men had not angered the god of the winds or the god of the sun. . . .*

Odysseus sighed with sorrow and despair. All his men were dead now, struck down by the wrath of the gods for their grievous sins. He alone had been spared. His strength and courage had helped him survive the horrors of war and the perils of his journey toward home.

Now Odysseus felt as if he were living in a nightmare from which he could not wake. For seven long years, the sea goddess Calypso had kept him captive on her island. Every day she tried to make him forget his past with her honey-sweet words. She promised him anything, if only he would marry her. She paid no heed to his protests that he still loved his true wife, Penelope, and their son, Telemachus.

And what is happening to my family now? Odysseus wondered.

He remembered the words the ghost of his mother had spoken when he journeyed to the Land of the Dead: "*Your family has been broken by sorrow. Your wife still waits for you. But she spends her days and nights weeping. Your son is strong and brave. Though he is young, he guards your home, your fields, and your livestock. He also mourns your absence, as does your father. . . .*"

It had been many years since his mother's spirit had spoken those words. Did his father still live? And what had become of his son? Telemachus had been a baby when Odysseus left Ithaca. Now he would be a young man of twenty.

And was Penelope still faithful? Or had she cast off all memory of Odysseus and married another?

Desperate to go back to Ithaca and be reunited with his family, Odysseus stared at the wine-dark waves and prayed for a ship to take him home.

Far, far away from Calypso's island, Odysseus' wife, Penelope, stood at her tower window listening to the rowdy suitors in the courtyard below.

Penelope shuddered. For the last four years, suitors had traveled from near and far, seeking her hand in marriage. She despised them all. She knew it was not her they truly wanted—it was Odysseus' farms and fields, his livestock and servants, his rule over the island.

When the suitors had first come, Penelope had thought of a clever plan to ward them off. She told them she could not remarry until she finished weaving a shroud for the Odysseus' father to wear when he died. Every day she sat at her loom, weaving the garment. But every night, by torchlight, she unraveled all her day's work.

For three years, Penelope carried out her deception, yearning for her husband to return. But in the fourth year, one of her maids told the suitors of her trick.

The suitors were furious. They demanded that Penelope pick one of them to be her new husband. Still, Penelope refused. None of the greedy, rude men could ever compare to her lost Odysseus.

Even after so many years, she could still clearly picture her beloved: his proud posture, his broad shoulders, his auburn hair and lively, darting eyes. She felt the spirit of Odysseus whenever she looked about their house—in the woodwork he had trimmed with silver and gold and ivory; in the special bed he had carved for them. Odysseus had built their bedroom around an olive tree. He had cut the limbs off the tree and used its trunk for one of the bedposts.

Only he and Penelope knew this secret.

Penelope desperately wished for Odysseus to return and take swift, fierce action against the villains who were trying to take his place. Without her husband, there was no one to protect her.

Odysseus' father was too aged and feeble to help. Lost in grief, the old man wandered the island, never coming near the palace.

Telemachus, Penelope's son, was too young to help her. He had his father's bright eyes and auburn hair, but not his strength or cunning. Lately, the suitors had grown more and more scornful of Telemachus. They had also grown angrier and more insistent that Penelope choose one of them for a husband.

As rude laughter came from the courtyard, Penelope closed the shutters of her window. She returned to her loom and began weaving.

Desperate for help, she prayed for her true husband to come home soon, before it was too late.

TWO

SON OF ODYSSEUS

Telemachus despised his mother's suitors even more than Penelope herself did. Every day, they invaded his father's estate. They slaughtered Odysseus' oxen, his long-horned cattle, his sheep, and his pigs. They stole wine from his vineyards and gave orders to his servants. Whenever Telemachus told them to leave, they laughed and mocked him.

Now, in the afternoon light, the suitors were sprawled about the courtyard, resting on the hides of oxen they had killed. They were playing dice and drinking from huge bowls of wine.

If my father would only come home, Telemachus thought, *he would quickly drive them all away and restore his rule over the island.*

Lost in his angry thoughts, Telemachus

did not notice for a moment that a stranger was waiting patiently at the threshold of the house. The stranger wore glittering gold sandals and carried a bronze spear.

When Telemachus finally saw the stranger, he jumped from his chair and hurried to welcome him. "Good day, sir!" he cried. "I am sorry you have been kept waiting at our gate!"

The stranger did not speak. He stared at Telemachus with piercing gray eyes.

"Come in, come in!" said Telemachus, ushering the stranger into the courtyard. "Refresh yourself with food and drink.

Then you must tell me from where you have come and what you seek."

Telemachus led the stranger quickly past the suitors in the courtyard and into the great hall. He wanted to protect his guest from the suitors' rudeness and noise.

"Please sit here," Telemachus said. He gestured to a tall, carved chair draped with the finest cloth. "Rest your feet on this stool."

Telemachus sat next to his guest. Servants brought trays of meat and bread. They poured wine and fresh water into golden goblets.

Soon Penelope's suitors began barging into the hall. They had come to hear music, sing songs, and dance. Telemachus was eager to ask questions of the visiting stranger, but he waited for the music to begin so the suitors would not hear his conversation.

As soon as the music and singing started, Telemachus leaned close to his gray-eyed guest.

"Tell me, sir, who are you?" the young man asked. "Where have you come from? What sort of ship brought you here? Are you a stranger to this house? Did you ever know my father, Odysseus, king of this island?"

"My name is Mentor," said the stranger. "I am chief of Taphos. Your father was a friend of mine, but I have not seen him since he left to fight the Trojan War. Recently I heard that he had come home, so I traveled here to Ithaca to see him again. I wanted to celebrate his safe return."

Telemachus lowered his head. "I am sorry to say my father has not returned," he said, "and we have had no word of him. I fear he has met with an ill fate and we shall never see him again."

"Perhaps the gods are only keeping him away for a while," said Mentor. "Perhaps he is a prisoner on an island somewhere. I am not a soothsayer, but deep within my heart, the gods whisper to me that your father is not dead. Remember, he is a man of great courage and strength. Even if he were in chains, he would eventually break free of them and find his way home."

Telemachus sighed. He dared not believe Mentor's words could be true. So many times over the years, his hopes about his father had been dashed.

The noise grew louder in the hall. All the suitors were singing now, and shouting, and making rude remarks.

Mentor looked at them. "Who are these men who swagger about your home?" he asked Telemachus. "Why do they behave in such a coarse and disgusting manner?"

"Sir, when my father was here, his estate was a safe and civilized place," said Telemachus. "But after he had been gone for some years, men from nearby islands began to invade our home. Now they slaughter and eat my father's livestock. They harass my mother and demand that she choose one of them to marry."

Mentor's eyes flashed with anger. "Odysseus must come home soon," he said in a low voice. "I have witnessed your father's strength. If he were here now, he would quickly punish these villains."

"Yes, I know he would," said Telemachus. "That is why I ache for his return. They will not listen to anything I say. I even fear they may soon try to kill me."

"My boy, you must gather your strength and courage," said Mentor, his voice shaking with anger. "You must find a way to deal with these men. Call them together tomorrow and order them to leave at once. Then gather a crew of twenty good men. Take the best ship you can find and set sail immediately in search of your father."

Telemachus was amazed by the vehemence of his guest. "I—I do not know how to search for him," he said.

"Sail to Pylos first," said Mentor. "Go to the home of wise Nestor. He was your father's friend and a brave warrior in the Trojan War. Ask Nestor about Odysseus. He will tell you what he knows, or he will tell you who else to ask."

"And what then?" asked Telemachus.

"If you learn that Odysseus has died, return home and mourn for him. Help your mother make plans to marry again. Kill those suitors who will not leave your estate."

Telemachus was frightened by the thought of such a challenge.

As if he could read Telemachus'

thoughts, Mentor leaned closer and looked deep into the young man's eyes. "Make a name for yourself, Telemachus," he said, "so people will praise your brave spirit. You are a man now, not a boy."

Telemachus felt heartened by the advice from Mentor. "Sir, you have been most kind to talk to me in this way," he said. "I feel almost as if you are my own father talking to me. I will do exactly as you say."

Mentor stood up to leave. "Now I must go back to my ship and crew," he said.

"Oh, please stay longer," implored Telemachus. "Rest, refresh yourself. Let me give you gifts to take with you."

"Nay, do not keep me," said Mentor. "I will receive your gifts when I stop here again. But now I must be on my way."

With these words, the gray-eyed stranger vanished as swiftly as a bird taking flight on the wind.

Telemachus was filled with wonder. He realized he'd been in the presence of a divine being.

THREE

THE GRAY-EYED GODDESS

Inspired by Mentor's words, Telemachus was determined to throw the suitors out of his house, once and for all.

They had quieted down a bit. A musician was playing his lyre and singing about the Greeks returning from the Trojan War. He sang about Athena's anger and how she had told the gods to punish the Greek warriors. He sang about the storms that had blown their ships off course.

As the man sang his sad song, Telemachus saw his mother come down the steep stairway from her chambers. Two loyal handmaidens walked behind her.

Penelope stood in the shadows, listening. Though her face was covered by a veil, Telemachus could see that she wept.

Before the song was over, she lifted

her veil. "Singer, sing a different song!" she cried out. "I cannot endure your tale. It breaks my heart."

Telemachus stepped over to his mother. Inspired by his talk with Mentor, he spoke in a strong, calm voice.

"Let him sing on, Mother," he said. "He is not the cause of our sorrow. Only Zeus can bring such grief to mankind. Go back upstairs to your loom. Do not worry about our estate. From now on, I will be the master of my father's house."

Penelope was astonished by Telemachus' bold and decisive words. "In this moment, you truly seem the son of Odysseus," she said.

Penelope began to weep again. Such a vivid reminder of her husband made her even more sorrowful than before.

As her handmaidens helped Penelope back up the stairs, the suitors shouted after her, begging her to choose one of them to marry.

Telemachus turned to them. "You are shameless!" he said. "Enjoy the music and dancing tonight. But tomorrow morning I shall command you to leave our house. From then on, you will steal from another table—not mine, and not my mother's."

Amazed by Telemachus' bold speech, the suitors did not speak at first. But when they recovered, they were quick to show they were not afraid. Antinous, leader of the suitors, smiled mockingly. "Such bold words, Telemachus," he said. "I pray the gods never make *you* ruler over this island."

Telemachus stood his ground. "Antinous, with the gods' blessings, I *will* have command over all that my father has fought for and won," he said.

"Let the heavens decide who will be

the rightful king of Ithaca, then," said another suitor. "But tell us about the stranger who was just here. From what country had he come? What family? Did he bring news of your father? He hurried away so quickly, we could not get to know him."

"He was Mentor, an old friend of my father," answered Telemachus. "He came to inquire about my father's return—which he believes will be very soon."

The suitors laughed and shook their heads. Then they turned back to the sweetly lulling music. Lost in their idle pleasure, they took no more heed of the son of Odysseus.

Telemachus left the great hall and headed toward his bedroom. His old nursemaid, Euryclea, carried two blazing torches to light his way.

Euryclea loved Telemachus as her own child, for she had cared for him since he was an infant. In his room, she prepared his bed and carefully put away his clothes. Then she left him alone with his thoughts.

Telemachus lay under a soft woolen fleece and stared into the dark. His mind burned with a question: *Is it possible that Mentor is the goddess Athena in disguise?*

Telemachus remembered the story told to him since he was a child: Before the Greeks had angered Athena, she had favored Odysseus above all other men. She had told him how to build the Trojan horse so the Greeks could lay siege to the city of Troy.

Had Athena finally taken pity on the man she had once loved? Had she disguised herself as Mentor and come to save Odysseus' wife and son?

After all, Mentor's bronze-tipped

spear was very like the spear of the goddess. His glittering gold sandals were like the magic sandals that carried her through the air.

And did not his gray eyes shine like the bright eyes of the goddess herself?

For the first time in months, Telemachus allowed hope to enter his heart. He felt certain the gray-eyed goddess had been with him today. She had come to help him find his father.

FOUR

SETTING SAIL

The next morning, Telemachus rose with the first light. In the rosy dawn, he dressed himself in his royal robe. He put on his sandals and strapped on his sword.

When he looked in his dressing

mirror, he was startled by his own appearance. He looked as handsome and powerful as a young god. Had Athena transformed him, he wondered, so he would shine before the others?

He bade his servants assemble all the men of Ithaca, including all the suitors. Then, with a spear in his hand and two hounds at his side, he went to meet the crowd.

As Telemachus moved through the throng of men, they all seemed to notice his changed appearance. Even the oldest among them made way for him.

Telemachus took his place at his father's seat and looked about at all those who had come to hear his words. As he rose to speak, he could hardly contain his emotions.

"You are demanding that my mother marry against her will," he said. "Day after day, you gather at this estate. You slaughter my father's livestock and drink his wine. He is not here to defend his home. I shall never be as strong a man as he was. Yet I cannot bear such treatment from you any longer. My father's house is falling into ruin—"

As Telemachus spoke, his newfound confidence began to fail him. "I—I ask you to respect your consciences and fear the wrath of heaven," he said in a trembling voice. Then, overpowered by his feelings, he dashed his spear to the ground and burst into tears.

From the looks on their faces, it seemed that some of the suitors had begun to feel true pity for Telemachus. The leader of the suitors, Antinous, stood up. "Blame your mother, Telemachus, not us," he said softly. "She deceived us. She said she could not choose a husband until she had woven a shroud for your grandfather. But every night she unraveled her day's work so the shroud would never be finished. For three years, she lied to us in this way. You must force her now to choose one of us to marry. We will not leave until she does."

Telemachus shook his head. "I cannot do as you say, Antinous," he said. "If you keep preying upon this house, I will ask Zeus for his help, and—and all of you will die."

As Telemachus spoke, a pair of eagles appeared overhead. Gliding on the currents of the wind, they circled the courtyard. Then they began furiously beating the air with their wings. They gave a death stare to those below. Then, suddenly, they turned on each other. They fought fiercely for a moment, then flew off into the sky.

The men murmured with alarm: "What can this mean? What is Zeus telling us?"

A wise old man stood up. He spoke in a shaky voice. "Men of Ithaca, I see an omen in the eagles," he said. "Zeus is telling us that Odysseus will not stay away much longer. Unless those who pursue his wife leave of their own accord, all our deaths are at hand. Let them be gone from this place before it is too late!"

But the suitors refused to heed the warning.

"Go home, old man!" one shouted. "Birds are always flying about! It means nothing! We shall stay here as long as we like! Odysseus is dead! We do not fear his son with his fine speeches!"

Telemachus shook his head. "The gods know my story," he said. "So here is what I propose to you. Give me a ship and a crew of twenty, and I shall set out in search of my father. If I hear that he is alive, we shall all wait patiently for his return. If I hear he is dead, we will have a funeral for him, and my mother will choose which one of you she will marry."

But the suitors would not agree even to this simple plan. Instead, they mocked Telemachus, saying he was not strong enough to survive such a voyage.

Then they returned to the halls of the palace to feast and drink while they waited for Penelope to make her choice.

In despair, Telemachus walked alone

down to the sea. He washed his hands in the foamy water and prayed to the goddess Athena for help.

"I know you came to me yesterday and bade me take a ship to search for my father," he said. "Tell me now what I should do! My mother's suitors scorn me! And now I fear no one in all of Ithaca will aid me in my quest."

In a flash, Mentor was at his side. His gray eyes glinting, he spoke plainly: "Telemachus, you have shown this morning that you indeed have a bit of your father's strength and courage. So I will help you on your journey. Think no more of the wicked ones who stand in your way. Believe me, on their day, they will pay for their rude disrespect. Return home, pack wine and provisions for your voyage to Nestor's island of Pylos. I will find men to sail with you. I will find the best ship and launch it upon the sea."

Telemachus thanked Mentor, and with great haste, he returned alone to his father's estate. When he arrived there, he found the suitors slaughtering goats and pigs in the courtyard.

They jeered at Telemachus as he passed by. "Boaster!" "Pretender!"

Telemachus ignored them and went straight to the storeroom where Odysseus kept his gold and bronze, and his finest clothes and oils and wines. Day and night, the storeroom was watched over by Telemachus' old nursemaid, Euryclea.

Telemachus now sought help from Euryclea. He asked her to pour wine into kegs and barley meal into bags.

"Keep these provisions hidden till nightfall," he told the old woman. "When it grows dark, I will collect them and take them to a ship that waits for me. I am sailing to Pylos tonight in search of news of my father. Promise not to tell my mother for at least ten days. If she knows my plan, she will try to stop me."

Euryclea cried out in distress. "Please do not go, my boy! These wicked men will be angry when they learn that you have left! They will find you and murder you!"

"No, I will be safe," Telemachus assured the old woman, "for this is the will of the goddess Athena. She is helping me."

Indeed, even as Telemachus spoke to Euryclea, the gray-eyed goddess was moving quickly about the city. Disguised as Telemachus himself, she found twenty good men to row his ship to Pylos.

When evening came and the streets were dark, Athena put a ship upon the sea and equipped it with all it needed for sailing. Then, disguised again as Mentor, she met the crew as they arrived at the dock.

Mentor set each man to work on the ship, then hurried to the house of Odysseus and put a spell of sleep upon all who were there, except Telemachus.

Still in the guise of Mentor, Athena

called to him from the great hall. "Your men and your ship are at the port. Let us go."

Telemachus hurried after Mentor. When he came to the shore, he found the crew of twenty waiting for him. With dignity and calm, the son of Odysseus gave them their orders: "Make haste to my house. Wake not a soul. No one else knows of our plan. Bring our provisions down to the shore."

Telemachus' crew quickly did as he ordered. Soon they were ready to cast off their anchor and set sail. Telemachus and Mentor took their seats in the stern of the vessel.

From the bright gray eyes of the goddess came a western wind. It rippled over the sea.

"Catch the ropes! Hoist the sail!" Telemachus called.

The crew lifted the mast and hauled up a white sail.

The wind blew full blast, and a dark wave sent the ship on its way. The men poured wine to honor the gods, most especially Athena, mighty daughter of Zeus.

Little do they know, thought Telemachus, *that the goddess herself sails with us tonight.*

FIVE

THE SEARCH

From dark till dawn, Telemachus' ship sped on its way toward King Nestor's island of Pylos.

Just as the sun was rising above the sea, the ship reached its port. A great crowd was gathered on the beach. They were offering sacrifices to Poseidon, lord of the seas.

The crew lowered their sail. Mentor ordered them to stay aboard, while he and Telemachus went ashore in search of King Nestor.

As they walked together, Mentor offered advice to the young man: "Do not be shy before the king," he said. "Ask him for news of your father—is he dead? And if so, where is he buried? Beg him to tell you the truth, for he is wise and powerful beyond all men."

Telemachus drew back, afraid to approach such a great man. King Nestor had been a fearless warrior and sailor, a master horseman, and a killer of giants. Most of all, he was known for his great wisdom and judgment.

"Do not worry," said Mentor. "Heaven will prompt you. Believe me when I tell you that the gods have been with you since the moment of your birth."

Hearing these words, Telemachus gathered his courage. When he and Mentor reached the crowd on the shore, they saw Nestor sitting with his seven sons as others prepared a great feast.

Two of Nestor's sons rushed forward to welcome the two strangers to their island. They invited them to sit on soft sheep-skins. They served them meat on silver platters and wine in golden cups.

When Mentor and Telemachus had finished eating and drinking, Nestor approached them. "It is proper to ask questions of guests only after they have had their fill of food and wine," he said. "So now that you have feasted with us, tell me: Who are you? From what land have you sailed? Are you traders or pirates?"

Mentor nodded to Telemachus, encouraging him to speak boldly.

"We come from Ithaca, the island once ruled by the brave Odysseus," Telemachus said. "We come in search of news of him. We want to learn of his fate when he sailed for home after the Trojan War. Please, tell us what you know. Do not soften the story. I must know the truth, for I am his son."

Nestor gasped with astonishment. "I can hardly believe my eyes," the old man said. "But now that you tell me who you are, I see that you indeed look very like your father, Odysseus. I will tell you all I know of his journeys and adventures.

"When we set sail from Troy, Athena was angry with some of the Greeks for defiling her temple in the heat of battle. At her bidding, Zeus scattered our fleet and flung our ships far away from each other on the open seas. I finally found my way back home, but knew nothing of the fate of my comrades. I could not say who had been saved or who had been lost. All I know of their fates is what I have since learned in the halls of my own palace. I am sorry, but no news of your father has ever come to me."

Telemachus sighed with despair. Then he told his father's old friend about the suitors who had invaded his home and were stealing his father's provisions.

Nestor was silent for a moment. He seemed deep in thought. Finally he spoke in a soft, steady voice.

"I will tell you what you should do now," he said. "Go to the palace of King Menelaus and beautiful Queen Helen. Menelaus was the last to arrive home from the Trojan War. He has traveled to many lands. Beg him to tell you all he knows. He will not deceive you."

Telemachus thanked Nestor for his counsel. Then Nestor invited Telemachus and Mentor to rest at his house for the night. "The son of mighty Odysseus and his friend need not sleep on the deck of a ship tonight!" he said.

Mentor stood up. "Thank you, but I fear I must return to our ship and take care of our crew. Telemachus will stay and sleep in your home. Please, lend him your swiftest horses and finest chariot, so that he might travel to the palace of Menelaus tomorrow."

Then, with these words, Athena suddenly took her leave—not as Mentor, but in the winged shape of a mighty eagle.

All who saw the sight were struck dumb with amazement. Nestor gasped and grabbed Telemachus' hand. "My friend," he said, "you travel with the gods themselves! I believe your friend was in truth the gray-eyed daughter of Zeus!"

Nestor prayed to Athena and promised to sacrifice a prized heifer in her honor. Then the old man led Telemachus to a lofty room of his palace where his servants had prepared a comfortable bed.

Telemachus rose early the next morning. He was bathed and anointed with oil. Then, dressed in a fine tunic and cloak, he left the palace of King Nestor to begin his journey.

Again, all who saw Telemachus were amazed, for he looked like a young god.

Nestor ordered that his swiftest horses be yoked to his finest chariot. He ordered his servants to pack provisions of meat, bread, and wine.

Then he bade his youngest son to travel with Telemachus to the palace of King Menelaus.

The two young men climbed into the chariot. Nestor's son took hold of the reins and snapped them sharply, and the team of horses galloped away.

All day the horses sped like the wind over the plains. When the sun went down and darkness spread over the land, they rested.

The next morning as dawn showed her rosy fingers in the sky, the two young men yoked the horses again and flew through fields of wheat and corn.

Again, the swift horses galloped all day. At nightfall, they came to a palace deep in a valley, the home of King Menelaus and beautiful Queen Helen.

SIX

THE OLD MAN OF THE SEA

The horses stopped at the gate of the palace. Telemachus and Nestor's son could hear sounds of a celebration coming from inside.

Servants greeted the two strangers at

the gate. The young men were welcomed and treated as grandly as royal visitors. Telemachus knew that this was the custom of all the Greeks. Wandering travelers received the greatest courtesy, for a man never knew when he himself might be a stranger in another's house.

Servants washed and anointed the two young men with sweet-smelling oil. They gave them the finest purple robes. Then they led them into the great hall.

Telemachus marveled at what he saw there. The splendor seemed greater than that of the sun or the moon.

Telemachus and Nestor's son were seated near the king. They were served rich foods and golden goblets filled with wine.

"Welcome," said King Menelaus. "Have your supper; then you shall tell me who you are and from where you have come."

As Telemachus ate, he looked about the great hall. The room gleamed with bronze, gold, and amber, and with ivory and silver.

"This palace seems like the very home of Zeus," he whispered to his friend.

King Menelaus overheard Telemachus' words. "Ah, I must not be compared with a god of Olympus," he said. "After the Trojan War, I traveled to many countries and gathered many treasures. But none of them take away the sorrow I still feel for my comrades who were slain by the Trojans, or who died on their voyages home.

"There is one I grieve for more than all the rest, for I have heard how his family still aches for his return. His mother died of her grief. His wife and his father have nearly gone mad with sorrow. Even his son mourns night and day for him, though the boy was but a babe when his father sailed away to war."

Telemachus covered his face to hide his tears. The king had perfectly described the family of Odysseus.

At that moment, Queen Helen came down from her perfumed room and entered the hall. Looking as beautiful as the most exquisite goddess, she took her seat beside the king.

"Who are these strangers?' she asked her husband. "Does not one of them look remarkably like the great Odysseus?"

Nestor's son nodded. "Indeed, this is the son of Odysseus," he said. "He is shy in your presence. My father, Nestor, has sent me with him to seek news of his father. In all Ithaca there is no one to help him fight the injustices he faces."

Menelaus was greatly moved to learn the identity of his young guest.

"Your father was much loved," he told Telemachus.

Then the king and queen, Telemachus, and even the son of Nestor wept for the lost warrior.

"He was a great warrior," said Helen.

"When I was held captive in Troy, it was his bravery and cunning that rescued me."

"Aye," said Menalaus. "I remember well how he dared to hide in the great wooden horse. Under the cover of night, he unlocked the gates of Troy, so we could lay siege to the city."

Telemachus nodded. "Your majesty, my father was very brave indeed," he said sadly, "but all his courage and cunning could not save him from his fate. Let us go to our beds now and seek peace from this sorrow in sleep."

Queen Helen ordered her maids to

make beds for the guests in the gallery of the palace. Servants led the two young men from the great hall by torchlight and offered them blankets and fine woolen gowns. Weary from their long journey, Telemachus and the son of Nestor finally lay down to rest.

Before dawn, Menelaus rose and went to the place where Telemachus slept. He woke the young man and spoke softly to him. "Tell me exactly why you came to see me in my palace," he said. "How can I help you?"

Telemachus told the king about the

suitors who had greedily moved into his father's home.

"If your father knew this," said Menelaus, "he would tear them to pieces."

"Do you have news of him?" asked Telemachus. "Can you tell me anything? Pray, do not soften your words."

"I will tell you what I know," said the king. "There is an island in the sea near Egypt where many voyagers stop to rest before sailing on. My ship landed there after the war. I was lost and did not know if any of my comrades had journeyed safely back home. One day, while

I was wandering alone, a sea nymph told me to speak to her father, the Old Man of the Sea."

"Who is he?" asked Telemachus.

"He is a sea god," said Menelaus. "He is Poseidon's herdsman, who tends to the seals. There is a time of day when he rises to the surface to count his flocks. To catch him, one must hold him fast, for he can change his shape into many forms. He can be any of the creatures that move about the earth. He can be water or fire. But if you can hold him fast, when he is himself again, you may ask him your questions."

"And did you catch this strange sea god?" Telemachus asked with wonder.

"Yes, I waited until he emerged to count his seals. Then I rushed upon him and seized him," said the king. "He quickly turned into a lion, then a snake, then a leopard, then a boar. He became running water, and then a tree. But I held him fast until he changed back into himself again. When I asked him how I might get home, he gave me wise advice.

"When I asked about the fate of my friends, he told me about those who had died. When I wept with grief, he told me that one great warrior was still alive. He said that Odysseus was trapped on the island of Calypso. The goddess was keeping him there against his will."

Telemachus rejoiced to hear that his father must still be alive.

Menelaus told him more about his journeys, then took his leave. Left alone, Telemachus was restless with excitement.

Is my father still on Calypso's island? he wondered. *Should I go in search of him there? Or should I return home at once and tell my mother the good news?*

SEVEN

CALYPSO'S ISLAND

Far away on Calypso's island, Odysseus sat on a rock and wept. On this day, like all others for the past seven years, he yearned for home.

With his face buried in his hands, he

did not see the bright light swoop through the air and skim the waves like a gull. He did not see Hermes, the messenger god, take shape before him.

Carrying his golden spear, and wearing his golden winged sandals, Hermes began moving lightly over the island. He stepped through Calypso's sacred woods, where owls, falcons, and seagulls called from the branches of alders, poplars, and cypresses.

He moved through Calypso's sweet-smelling garden, over beds of violets and herbs. Finally he came to the entrance of the goddess's cave.

Hermes pushed past the hanging grape vines and stepped inside. The scent of cedar and sandalwood filled the air.

The fair-haired goddess was sitting at her loom before her hearth, singing a song. When she looked up, she gave the messenger god a radiant smile.

"Hermes, you have honored me with a visit!" she said. "Sit and let me offer you food and drink."

Calypso served Hermes ambrosia and red nectar, food for the gods. After he had refreshed himself, Hermes told Calypso the purpose of his visit.

"Today on Olympus, the goddess Athena called together all the gods," he said. "She is greatly worried about Odysseus, king of Ithaca. He has been kept from his home and family too long, she says, and now his enemies are planning to murder his son. Calypso, Zeus has heard the words of his daughter. He commands you to release your captive."

The goddess rose in anger, but Hermes continued: "Zeus has decreed that Odysseus must return home on his own strength. No god is allowed to speed his journey. He must build a raft and ride the waves for twenty days to the land of Scheria. From there, he can sail on to Ithaca and avenge the wrongs done to his family."

"The gods of Olympus are angry with me," said Calypso. "They do not like to believe a goddess can fall in love with a mortal man! But I saved Odysseus' life!"

Calypso stared fiercely at Hermes for a moment. Then she lowered her eyes in defeat. "I know I cannot defy the will of Zeus," she said. "If Zeus commands it, Odysseus shall leave my island. In all good faith, I will give him the advice he needs to begin his journey home."

Hermes bowed. Then he took swift leave of the mournful goddess.

Calypso set out to look for Odysseus. She found him on the rocks, weeping. She sat beside him and spoke gently.

"You shall no longer stay here, yearning for your home," she said. "I will send you away. Go, cut beams of wood. Make a large raft to carry you over the sea. I will give you wine, bread, water, and clothing."

After his many years of being held captive, Odysseus did not trust

Calypso's words. "Not even a well-made ship could safely sail these waves," he said. "Will you swear a sacred oath that you are not trying to harm me?"

The goddess took his hand. "I swear by heaven and earth and by the waters of the Underworld that I want no harm to come to you, Odysseus," she said.

Having sworn her oath, Calypso rose and quickly walked away. Odysseus followed her to her cave. Calypso bade her servants prepare a meal. Her handmaidens served her ambrosia and nectar, food for the deathless gods. Calypso herself served Odysseus meat and wine, refreshment for mere mortals.

"Odysseus, if you would only promise to stay with me and marry me, I would make you, too, an immortal being," Calypso said. "You would live forever."

"Fair goddess, why would I want to live forever far from my home, without my wife and son?" he asked.

"I cannot imagine that your wife is more beautiful than I am," said Calypso.

"Goddess, do not be angry with me," said Odysseus. "What you say is true.

My wife is a mortal woman. She is not as beautiful as you. Still, for seven years, I have thought of nothing but getting home to her."

Desperate to keep Odysseus on her island, Calypso gave him one more reason to stay. "If you sail for home, Odysseus, you will find many troubles along the way, for the gods will not aid your journey," she said. "They will test your powers of endurance, again and again."

"Should the gods choose to destroy my raft, I shall bear it," said Odysseus.

"I have suffered many hardships and can certainly endure one more."

Calypso sighed and nodded. She could see that she had no choice. She had to let Odysseus go.

The next morning, at dawn, Calypso dressed in a beautiful shimmering silver gown. She covered her head with a veil. Then she gave Odysseus a sharp ax made of bronze and led him to the far end of the island.

There, many tall trees grew—aspens and pines that reached as high as the sky.

"Cut what you need for your ship," the goddess said.

For the next four days, Odysseus cut down trees with his bronze ax. He worked until he had felled twenty. Then he set about building his raft.

He smoothed the felled timbers and fixed them together with wooden bolts. Then he built a deck and made a mast and a steering rudder. Calypso gave him linen cloth for a sail. When the sea craft was finally finished, Odysseus used logs to roll it down to the water.

On the fifth day after Hermes' visit

to Calypso, Odysseus was ready to set sail. Calypso gave him clean clothes. She gave him goatskins filled with deep-red wine and water and meat. She told him which stars he should follow to guide his way.

The goddess hid her grief as Odysseus moved away from her into the water and climbed aboard his raft.

The last gift Calypso gave Odysseus was a fair, warm wind to send his raft safely out to sea.

EIGHT

THE VOYAGE

With his hands gripping the rudder, Odysseus skillfully guided his raft over the waves. He never slept. All night, he kept his eyes fixed on the stars that Calypso had told him to watch—the Pleiades and the Bear.

Day after day and night after night, Odysseus sailed the seas. Finally, on the eighteenth day, he saw the dim outline of mountains on the horizon.

As Odysseus steered his raft toward the shore, dark clouds gathered over-head. The water began to rise. The wind began to blow, until it was roaring over the earth and sea.

Has Poseidon discovered my raft? Odysseus wondered anxiously. *Does he now seek his final revenge?*

For many years, Poseidon, mighty

ruler of the sea, had been angry with Odysseus for blinding his son, the Cyclops. Now it seemed he was trying to destroy Odysseus once again. The wind roared from the north, south, east, and west. Daylight plunged into darkness. Odysseus feared he was about to come to a terrible, lonely end.

Suddenly an enormous wave crashed down on Odysseus' raft. Odysseus was swept overboard and pulled deep beneath the sea. He struggled wildly to raise his head above the water and breathe.

When his head finally broke the

surface, Odysseus saw his raft swiftly moving away across the water. He swam as fast as he could toward the wooden craft. He grabbed the timbers and pulled himself aboard.

Then, as the wind swirled the raft across the water, Odysseus saw an astonishing sight. A sea goddess was floating like a gull on top of the waves.

Seemingly impervious to the great storm, she floated near his raft and climbed aboard.

"My friend," she said, "I am Ino, the White Goddess, who guides sailors in storms. I know not why Poseidon is angry with you. But I know this: for all the torture he has inflicted upon you, he will not kill you. But you must leave your raft at once and swim for the shore. Take my veil, for it is enchanted. You will come to no harm as long as you possess it. As soon as you reach land, you must throw it back into the sea."

With these words, the White Goddess removed her enchanted veil and gave it to Odysseus. Then she disappeared back into the wild seas.

At that moment, a huge wave crashed

down on Odysseus' raft, ripping it to pieces. Clutching Ino's veil, Odysseus pulled himself onto a wooden plank and rode it as if it were a horse. Then he dove down into the sea.

Suddenly, all the winds died down—except the north wind. Odysseus felt that Athena was holding the other winds back, so he could swim safely and swiftly to some distant shore. For two days and two nights, with the north wind gently flattening the waves before him, he swam and floated on the calm sea.

On the third day, the north wind

died away and the sea was completely calm. Odysseus saw land ahead. With a burst of joy, he swam toward the rocky shore.

In an instant, the wind and waves returned. With a thundering roar, sea spray rained down on him.

Odysseus struggled to keep his head above the churning water, seeking a place to go ashore.

Angry waves were pounding the reefs with great force. *I'll be dashed against the rocks if I try to swim ashore now*, he thought desperately.

But once again, Odysseus felt the presence of Athena. A giant wave picked him up and carried him over the rocks toward the beach. But before Odysseus could crawl ashore to safety, another wave dragged him back into the sea and pulled him under the water.

Odysseus swam desperately, escaping the waves pounding the shore. Soon he came to a sheltered cove. He saw a riverbank free of rough stones. As he swam toward the bank, he prayed to the gods to save him from the angry attack of Poseidon.

Suddenly the waves were still. But when Odysseus tried to haul himself ashore, his body failed him. He had been defeated by the storm. It had ripped his flesh and robbed his muscles of their strength. He was passing in and out of consciousness.

Gasping for breath, he pulled off Ino's veil and threw it back into the sea. Then he used his last bit of strength to drag himself out of the water and throw himself into the river reeds.

If I lie here all night, I shall die from the cold and damp, he thought. *If I go farther ashore and pass out in a thicket, wild beasts will devour me.* No matter what evils lay ahead, he knew he had to push on. On bleeding hands and knees, he crawled to a sheltered spot under an olive tree, a tree sacred to the goddess Athena.

Odysseus lay down in a pile of dead leaves. With his bloody hands, he spread leaves over his torn body. Like a farmer spreading ashes over the embers of his fire, he tried to protect the last spark of life within him.

Mercifully, the gray-eyed goddess slipped down from the heavens and appeared at his side. She closed his weary eyes and pulled him down into a sweet sleep that took away his pain and sorrow.

EPILOGUE

Back in Ithaca, Penelope, the wife of Odysseus, opened her door and greeted a friend named Medon.

"I have just received terrible news," said Medon. "Your suitors, led by Antinous, are plotting against your son. They are waiting for him on the island of Asteris. When his ship sails past, they will kill him."

Penelope fell to the floor in a faint. When she came to, she wept bitterly. "Where is my boy?" she said between sobs. "I thought he was somewhere in the countryside."

"I know only that he set out some days ago in search of news of his father," said Medon. "Soon he will be sailing for home and crossing the path of his enemies."

Penelope was plunged into such despair that she could not rise from the floor. As she wept and wailed for her lost husband and her beloved son, all her handmaidens wept with her.

Euryclea, the aged nursemaid of Telemachus, tried to comfort her. "Call upon the goddess Athena!" she urged Penelope. "Ask for her help. She will save your boy!"

The old woman wiped away Penelope's tears. She helped her bathe and dressed her in clean linens. She helped her make an offering to the goddess.

Penelope prayed to Athena. "O daughter of Zeus, hear me," she said. "I beg you to keep my son safe from harm."

Exhausted and filled with grief,

Penelope then went to her chambers and lay down on her bed.

Mercifully, the gray-eyed goddess soon came. She closed Penelope's weary eyes and pulled her down into a sweet sleep that took away her pain and sorrow.

ABOUT HOMER AND THE *ODYSSEY*

Long ago, the ancient Greeks believed that the world was ruled by a number of powerful gods and goddesses. Stories about the gods and goddesses are called the Greek myths. The myths were probably first told as a way to explain things in nature—such as weather, volcanoes, and constellations. They were also recited as entertainment.

The first written record of the Greek myths comes from a blind poet named Homer. Homer lived almost three thousand years ago. Many believe that Homer was the author of the world's two most famous epic poems: the *Iliad* and the *Odyssey.* The *Iliad* is the story of the Trojan War. The *Odyssey* tells about the long journey of Odysseus, king of an island called Ithaca. The tale concerns Odysseus' adventures on his way home from the Trojan War.

To tell his tales, Homer seems to have drawn upon a combination of his own imagination and Greek myths that had been passed down by word of mouth. A bit of actual history may have also gone into Homer's stories; there is archaeological evidence to suggest that the story of the Trojan War was based on a war fought about five hundred years before Homer's time.

Over the centuries, Homer's *Odyssey* has greatly influenced the literature of the Western world.

GODS AND GODDESSES OF ANCIENT GREECE

The most powerful of all the Greek gods and goddesses was Zeus, the thunder god. Zeus ruled the heavens and the mortal world from a misty mountaintop known as Mount Olympus. The main Greek gods and goddesses were all relatives of Zeus. His brother Poseidon was ruler of the seas, and his brother Hades was ruler of the underworld. His wife

Hera was queen of the gods and goddesses. Among his many children were the gods Apollo, Mars, and Hermes, and the goddesses Aphrodite, Athena, and Artemis.

The gods and goddesses of Mount Olympus not only inhabited their mountaintop but also visited the earth, involving themselves in the daily activities of mortals such as Odysseus.

THE MAIN GODS AND GODDESSES AND PRONUNCIATION OF THEIR NAMES

Zeus (zyoos), king of the gods, god of thunder

Poseidon (poh-SY-don), brother of Zeus, god of seas and rivers

Hades (HAY-deez), brother of Zeus, king of the Land of the Dead

Hera (HEE-ra), wife of Zeus, queen of the Olympian gods and goddesses

Hestia (HES-tee-ah), sister of Zeus, goddess of the hearth

Athena (ah-THEE-nah), daughter of Zeus, goddess of wisdom and war, arts and crafts

Demeter (dih-MEE-tur), goddess of crops and the harvest, mother of Persephone

Aphrodite (ah-froh-DY-tee), daughter of Zeus, goddess of love and beauty

Artemis (AR-tem-is), daughter of Zeus, goddess of the hunt

Ares (AIR-eez), son of Zeus, god of war

Apollo (ah-POL-oh), god of the sun, music, and poetry

Hermes (HUR-meez), son of Zeus, messenger god, a trickster

Hephaestus (heh-FEES-tus), son of Hera, god of the forge

Persephone (pur-SEF-uh-nee), daughter of Zeus, wife of Hades and queen of the Land of the Dead

Dionysus (dy-oh-NY-sus), god of wine and madness

PRONUNCIATION GUIDE TO OTHER PROPER NAMES

Agamemnon (ag-ah-MEM-non)

Asteris (ahss-TER-iss)

Calypso (cah-LIP-soh)

Cyclops (SY-klops)

Euryclea (yoor-ih-KLAY-ah)

Ino (EYE-noh)

Ithaca (ITH-ah-kah)

Medon (MEE-don)

Menelaus (men-eh-LAY-us)

Mentor (MEN-tor)

Nestor (NES-tor)

Odysseus (oh-DIS-yoos)

Penelope (pen-EL-oh-pee)

Pylos (PY-lohs)

Scheria (SKER-ee-ah)

Taphos (TA-fohss)

Telemachus (Tel-EM-ah-kus)

Trojans (TROH-junz)

A NOTE ON THE SOURCES

The story of the *Odyssey* was originally written down in the ancient Greek language. Since that time there have been countless translations of Homer's story into other languages. I consulted a number of English translations, including those written by Alexander Pope, Samuel Butler, Andrew Lang, W. H. D. Rouse, Edith Hamilton, Robert Fitzgerald, Allen Mandelbaum, and Robert Fagles.

Homer's *Odyssey* is divided into twenty-four books. The fourth volume of *Tales from the Odyssey* was derived from books one through five, and part of book fifteen, of Homer's *Odyssey.*

ABOUT THE AUTHOR

MARY POPE OSBORNE is the author of the best-selling Magic Tree House series. She has also written many acclaimed historical novels and retellings of myths and folktales, including *Kate and the Beanstalk* and *New York's Bravest.* She lives with her husband in New York City and Connecticut.

Zeus
Hera
Artemis
Hephaestus
Apollo
Athena
Ares